W9-ASU-807

Jesus Himself referenced His church as a city on a hill, a beacon of welcoming brightness and truth to the world. This story (and the song that inspired it) depicts that body of Christ. The storyline was inspired by 1 Corinthians 12 where the apostle Paul recognized the differences in us all. Some are hands, some are eyes, but we each serve a distinct and important purpose and are interdependent within the church.

City on the Hill opens with two old men reminiscing about the city. As they weave their stories, they remember how the soldiers thought the poets were weak and the elders saw the young people as foolish. Each group had no appreciation for the talents and purposes of the others. As a result, everyone abandoned the city, and the city fell into disrepair. It's an allegory of the people in the church today, the result of predominantly like-minded people often dwelling upon nonessentials and personal taste to go their own directions.

This message is of critical importance for children today. Early on, they need to learn and understand that God designed each of them with different personalities and talents. He also designed them to work together for His glory. It is our prayer that this story will help to teach children that only by working together can we forge a lasting impact for God's kingdom.

–Mark Hall

Copyright © 2014 by Mark Hall. All Rights Reserved.
"City on the Hill" Written by Mark Hall & Matthew West © 2011 My Refuge Music (BMI)
(adm. at CapitolCMGPublishing.com) / External Combustion Music (ASCAP) / Sony/Atv Tree Pub (BMI)
All rights reserved. Used by permission.
Illustrations Copyright © 2013 by B&H Publishing Group, Nashville, Tennessee.
Scripture quotations are taken from the Holman Christian Standard Bible®,
Copyright © 1999, 2000, 2002, 2003, 2009 by Holman Bible Publishers.

ISBN: 978-1-4336-8231-5
Dewey Decimal Classification: C262.7
Subject Heading: CHURCH—UNITY \ COOPERATIVENESS \ CHRISTIAN LIFE
Printed in China.
1 2 3 4 5 6 7 8 - 18 17 16 15 14

Mark Hall &
Matthew West

Based on the hit song by
CASTING CROWNS

CITY ON THE HILL

B&H KIDS
Nashville, Tennessee

"Did you hear of the city on the hill?"
Said one old man to the other.

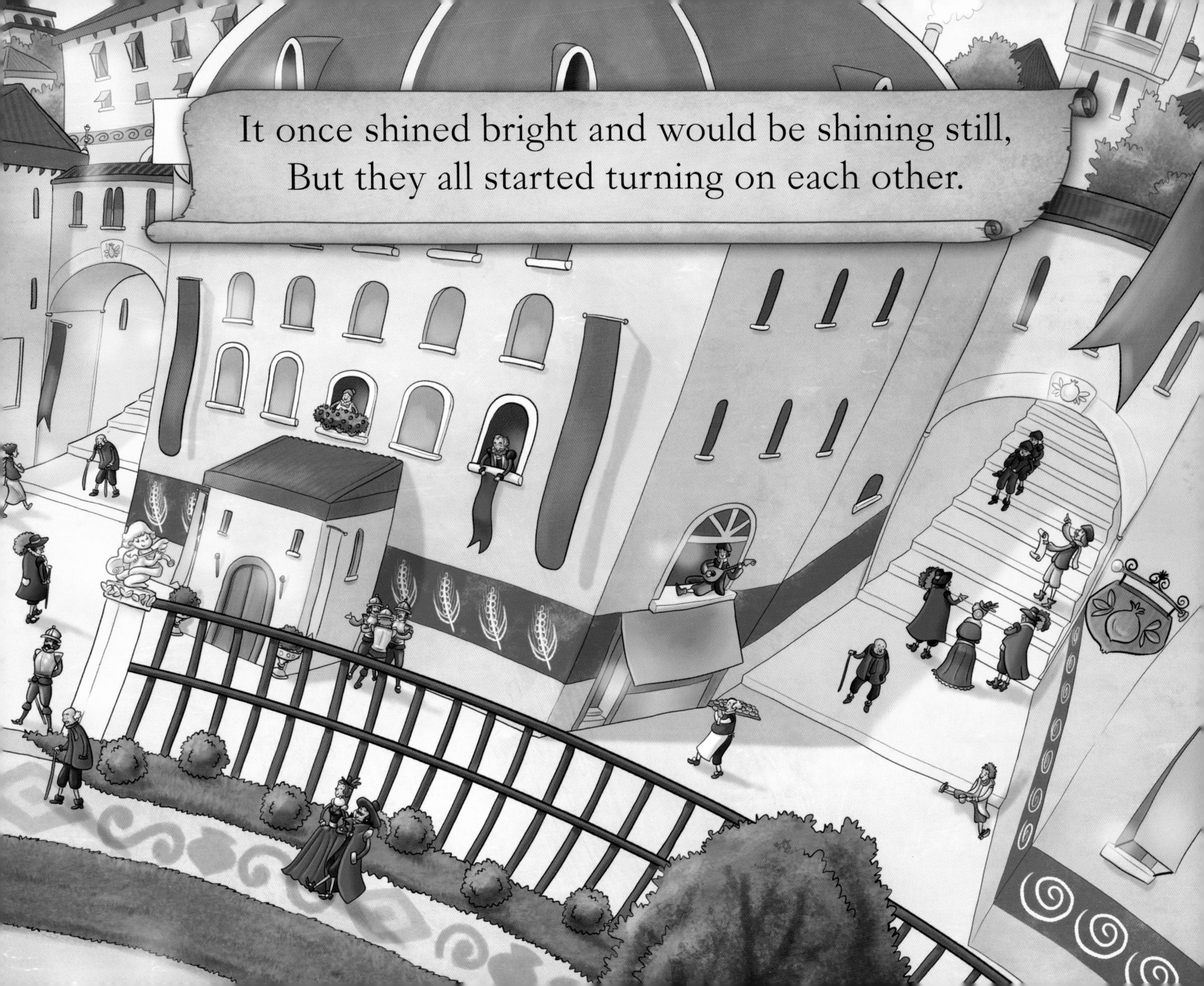
It once shined bright and would be shining still,
But they all started turning on each other.

You see, the poets thought the dancers were shallow …

And the soldiers thought
the poets were weak.

And the elders saw
the young ones as foolish . . .

And the rich man never
heard the poor man speak.
Apprentice
Wanted

Each one thought that they knew better,
But they were different by design.

Instead of standing strong together,
They let their differences divide.

And one by one, they ran away,
With their made up minds, to leave it all behind.

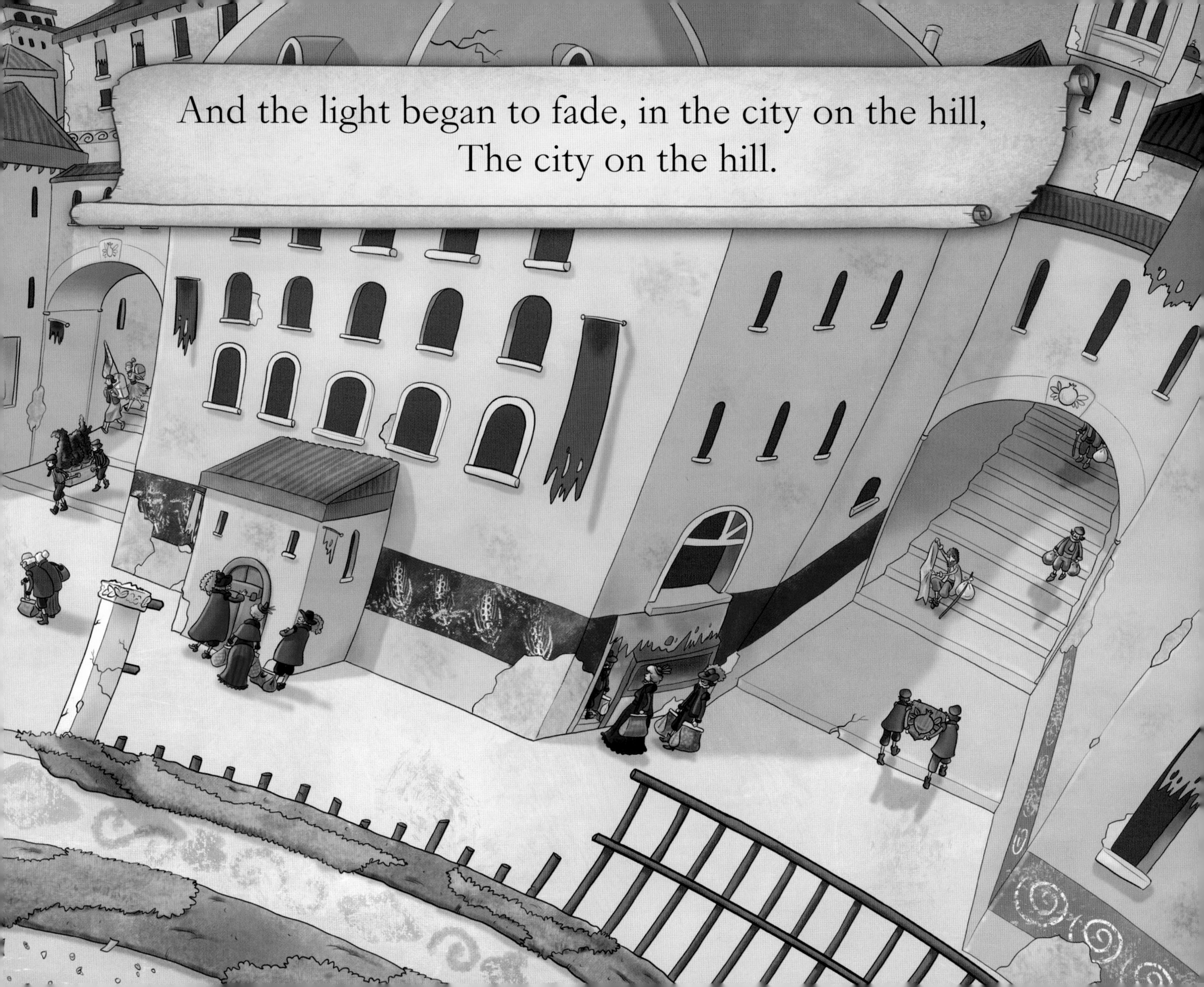
And the light began to fade, in the city on the hill,
The city on the hill.

And the world

is searching still.

It is the rhythm of the dancers
that gives the poets life.

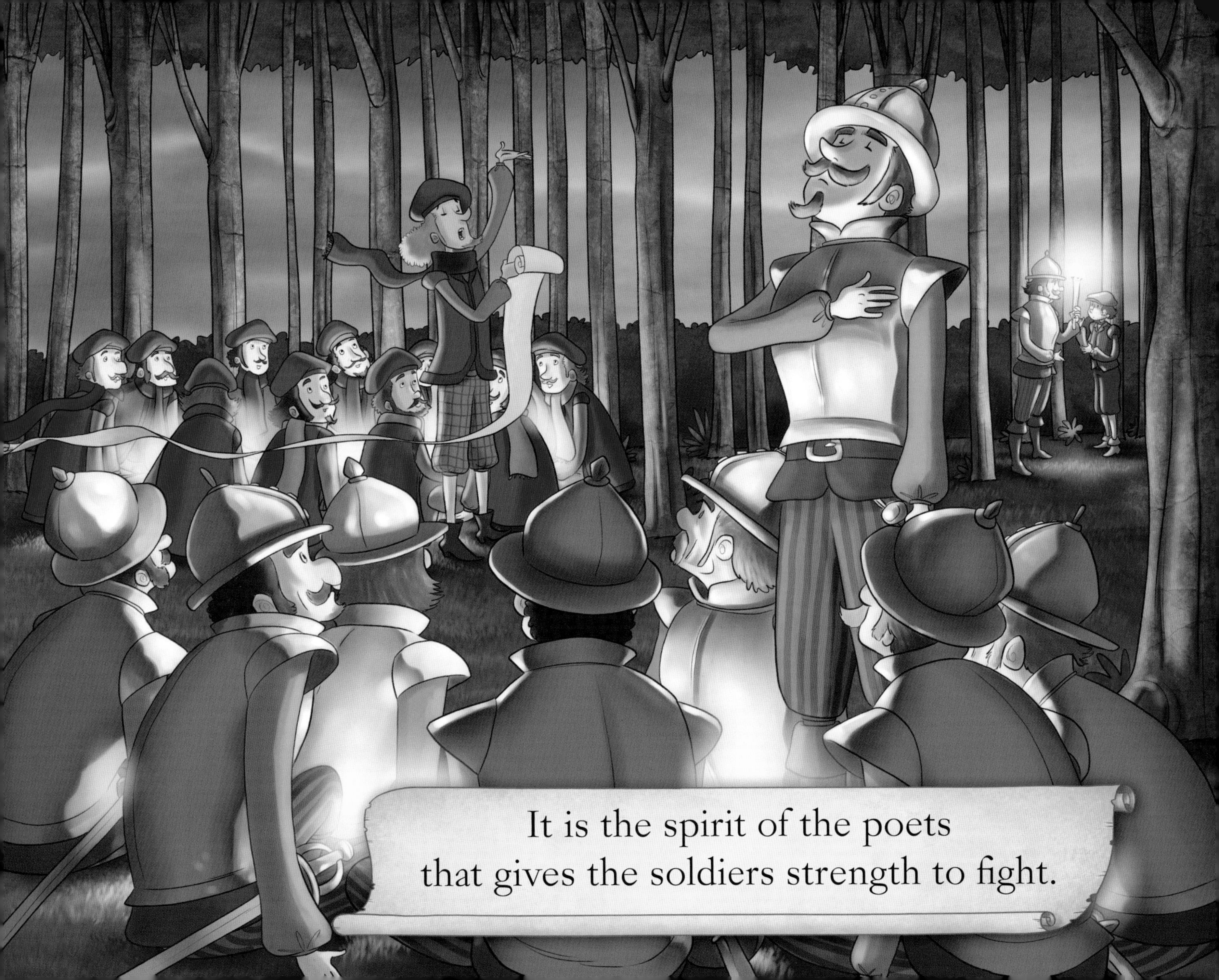

It is the spirit of the poets
that gives the soldiers strength to fight.

It is the fire of the young ones;
it is the wisdom of the old.

It is the story of the poor man
that's needing to be told.

Come home . . . The

Father's calling still.

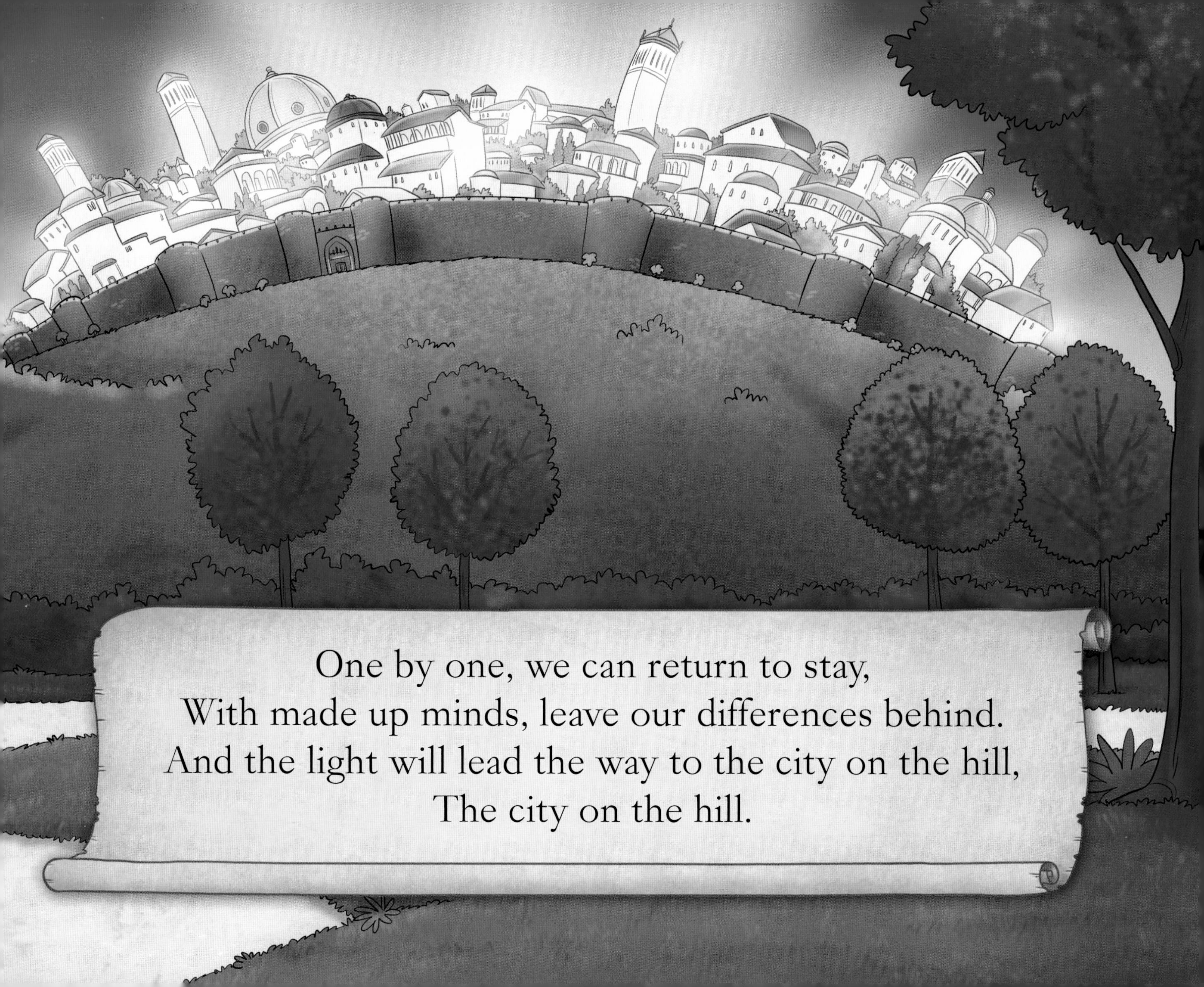

One by one, we can return to stay,
With made up minds, leave our differences behind.
And the light will lead the way to the city on the hill,
The city on the hill.

Come home …
To the city on the hill.

Come home.